YOU'RE THE VOICE
Billie Holiday

CW00496422

14·99

© 2008 by International Music Publications Ltd
First published by International Music Publications Ltd in 2004
International Music Publications Ltd is a Faber Music company
Bloomsbury House
74–77 Great Russell Street
London WC1B 3DA

Editorial, Production and Recording by Artemis Music Limited
Original design by IMP Studio
Photography by Herman Leonard/Redferns

Printed in England by Caligraving Ltd
All rights reserved

ISBN10: 0-571-53282-9
EAN13: 978-0-571-53282-7

Reproducing this music in any form is illegal and forbidden
by the Copyright, Designs and Patents Act, 1988

To buy Faber Music publications or to find out about the full range of titles available,
please contact your local music retailer or Faber Music sales enquiries:

Faber Music Ltd, Burnt Mill, Elizabeth Way, Harlow, CM20 2HX England
Tel: +44(0)1279 82 89 82   Fax: +44(0)1279 82 89 83
sales@fabermusic.com   fabermusicstore.com

Billie Holiday
Born 7th April 1915
Died 17th July 1959

Generally recognised as the greatest of all jazz singers, Billie Holiday had what might be described as a 'difficult' childhood. Abandoned firstly by her father and then left in the care of relatives when her mother moved to New York, her early musical influences were Louis Armstrong and Bessie Smith.

Moving to New York in 1928 to be with her mother, she started singing in clubs frequented by jazz enthusiasts and quickly came to the attention of producer John Hammond. Her first recording sessions were with Benny Goodman, and subsequent records included many works by Lester Young. Such was the influence of these songs that her style was soon being recreated throughout America.

In the late 1930s she featured with Count Basie and Artie Shaw and then began singing at Café Society, an engagement that brought about more popular appreciation. Although not a true singer of the Blues, she had particular success with melancholic love songs and by the end of the 1940s was a world-wide star. Despite this, her personal life was less than stable and she was jailed in 1947 after standing trial on charges of drug use. This inevitably affected her health and, in course, her voice, although she continued to perform and record until the mid 1950s. She died in Philadelphia on 17th July 1959.

Billie Holiday had a significant influence on many later singers, and although her voice was untrained she had an excellent musical ear. Her style of delivery – stretching or pulling back the natural position of the beat to great extremes – owing much to the influence of Louis Armstrong.

"I can't stand to sing the same song the same way two nights in succession, let alone two years or ten years. If you can, then it ain't music, it's close-order drill or exercise or yodeling or something, not music."

All Of Me

Words and Music by Seymour Simons and Gerald Marks

Track 1
Backing

Moderately ♩ = 108

Lyrics: All of me, why not take all of me, can't you see__ I'm no good with-out you?__

© 1931 (renewed) Bourne Co and Marlong Music, USA
Bourne Music Ltd, London W1B 4ND and Redwood Music Ltd, London NW1 8BD
All Rights Reserved. International Copyright Secured.

Body And Soul

Words by Frank Eyton, Edward Heyman and Robert Sour
Music by Johnny Green

Backing

© 1930 Harms Inc, USA
Warner/Chappell Music Ltd, London W6 8BS

God Bless The Child

Words and Music by Billie Holiday and Arthur Herzog Jr

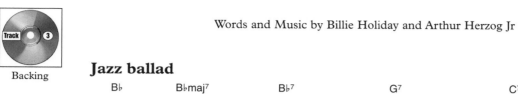

Jazz ballad

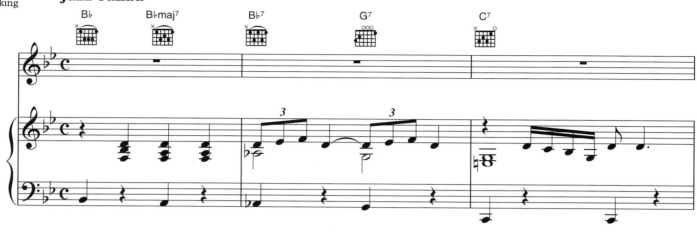

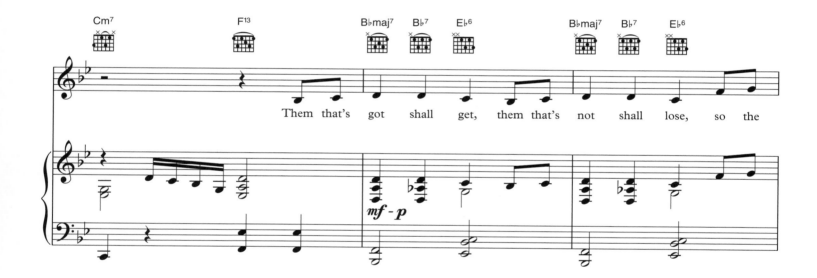

Them that's got shall get, them that's not shall lose, so the

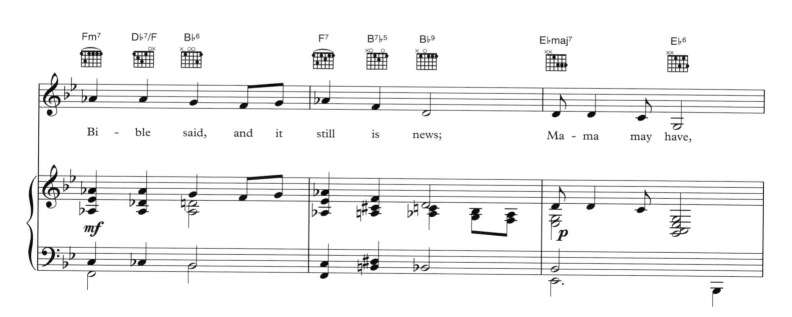

Bi - ble said, and it still is news; Ma - ma may have,

© 1941 Edward B. Marks Music Co, USA
Carlin Music Corp, London NW1 8BD

Billie's Blues (I Love My Man)

Words and Music by Billie Holiday

Medium boogie tempo

Lord I love my man   tell the world I   do___

© 1936 Edward B. Marks Music Co, USA
Carlin Music Corp, London NW1 8BD

Lady Sings The Blues

Words and Music by Herbert Nichols and Billie Holiday

Backing

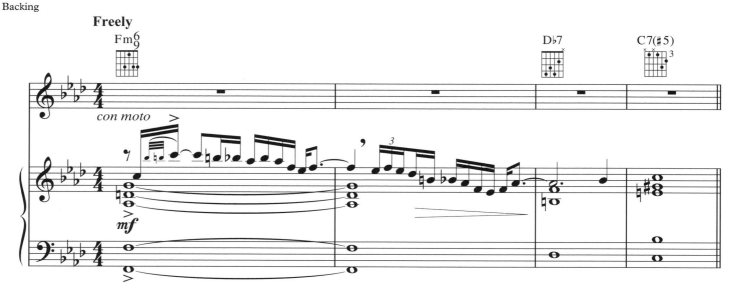

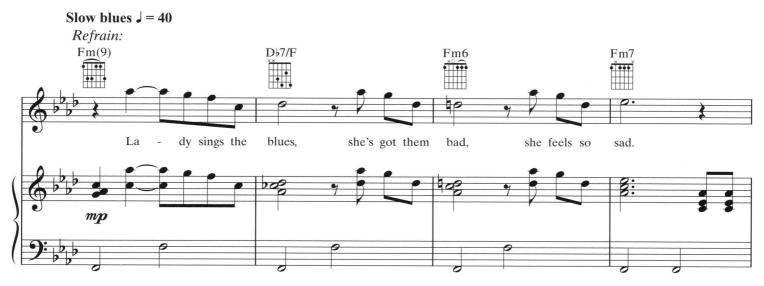

Lady sings the blues, she's got them bad, she feels so sad.

And wants the world to know just what her blues is all a-bout.

© 1956 MCA-Northern Music Co Inc, USA
Universal/MCA Music Ltd, London SW6 4FX

Lover Man (Oh Where Can You Be)

Track 6

Backing

Words and Music by Jimmy Davis, Roger Ramirez and James Sherman

Steady tempo

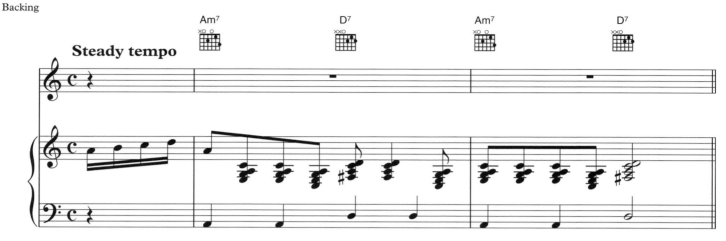

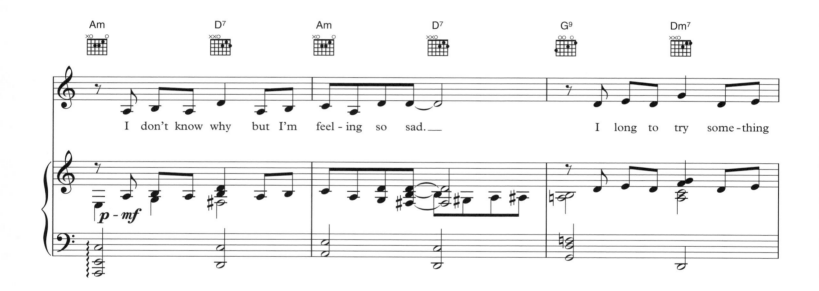

I don't know why but I'm feel-ing so sad.___ I long to try some-thing

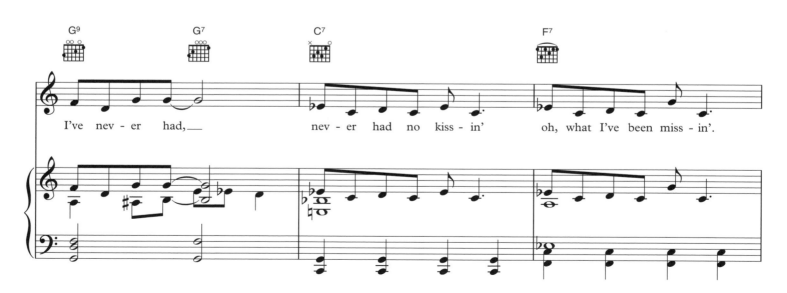

I've nev-er had,___ nev-er had no kiss-in' oh, what I've been miss-in'.

© 1942 MCA Inc, USA
Universal/MCA Music Ltd, London SW6 4FX

The Man I Love

Music and Lyrics by George Gershwin and Ira Gershwin

© 1924 (renewed) Chappell & Co Inc, USA
Warner/Chappell Music Ltd, London W6 8BS

My Man ('Mon Homme')

Original Words by Jacques Charles
English Words by Channing Pollock
Music by Maurice Yvain

Backing

Ballad tempo (rubato)

It's cost me a lot, but there's

one thing that I've got, it's my man,____ it's my man,____ cold and

wet, tired you bet, all of this I'll soon for-get with my man.____ He's

© 1921 Editions Salabert S.A., France
Ascherberg Hopwood & Crew Ltd, London W6 8BS

Night And Day

Words and Music by Cole Porter

Backing

Moderato

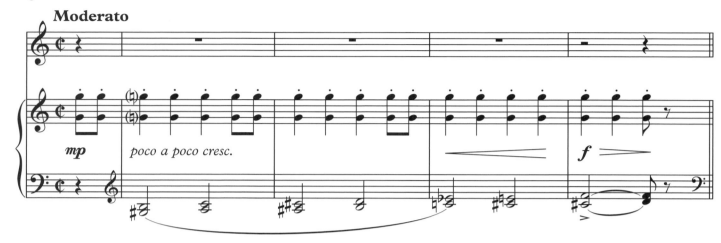

Verse

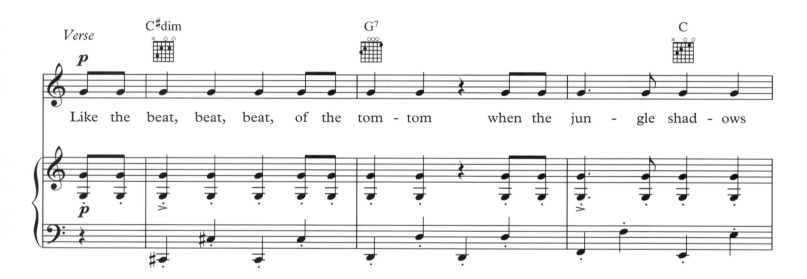

Like the beat, beat, beat, of the tom - tom when the jun - gle shad - ows

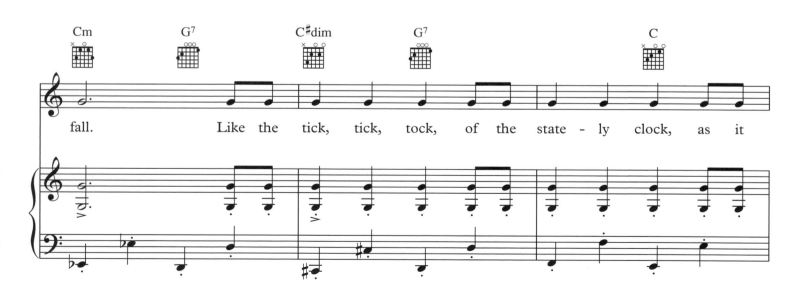

fall. Like the tick, tick, tock, of the state - ly clock, as it

© 1932 Harms Inc, USA
Warner/Chappell Music Ltd, London W6 8BS

35

St. Louis Blues

Words and Music by William C. Handy

© 1914 Handy Brothers Music Co Inc, USA
Francis Day & Hunter Ltd, London WC2H 0QY

YOU'RE THE VOICE

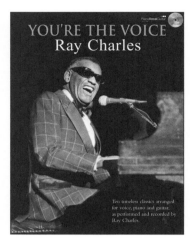
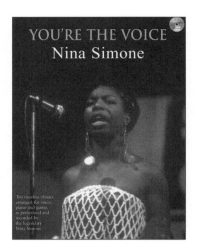

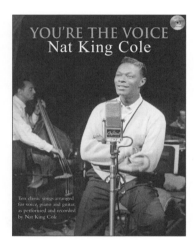
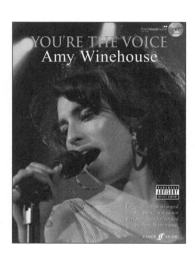
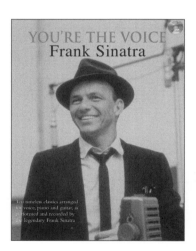

The outstanding vocal series from Faber Music
CD contains full backings for each song,
professionally arranged to recreate the sounds of the original recording

Shirley Bassey · James Blunt · Michael Bublé · Maria Callas · Eva Cassidy · Ray Charles
Nat King Cole · Sammy Davis Jr · Celine Dion · Ella Fitzgerald · Aretha Franklin · Billie Holiday
Katherine Jenkins · Norah Jones · Tom Jones · Alicia Keys · Carole King · Madonna
George Michael · Dean Martin · Bette Midler · Matt Monro · Nina Simone
Frank Sinatra · Dusty Springfield · Barbra Streisand · Amy Winehouse

Faber *ff* MUSIC

To buy Faber Music publications or to find out about the full range of titles available
please contact your local music retailer or Faber Music sales enquiries:

Faber Music Ltd, Burnt Mill, Elizabeth Way, Harlow CM20 2HX
Tel: +44 (0) 1279 82 89 82   Fax: +44 (0) 1279 82 89 83
sales@fabermusic.com   fabermusic.com   fabermusicstore.com

all woman

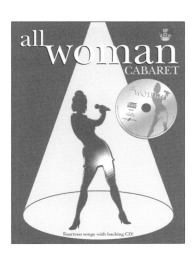
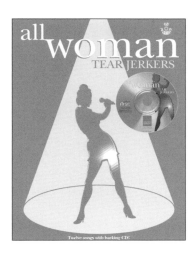

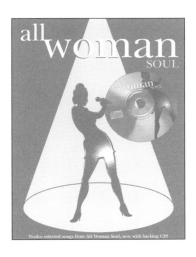
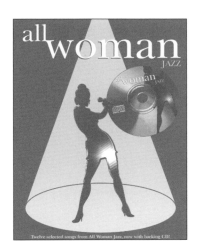
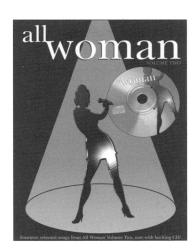

All Woman Collection. Vol.1 WITH CD   All Woman. Love Songs WITH CD
All Woman Collection. Vol.2 WITH CD   All Woman. Jazz WITH CD
All Woman Collection. Vol.3 WITH CD   All Woman. Blues WITH CD
All Woman Collection. Vol.4 WITH CD   All Woman. Soul WITH CD
All Woman. Songbirds WITH CD   All Woman. Cabaret WITH CD
All Woman. Power Ballads WITH CD   All Woman Tearjerkers WITH CD
All Woman Bumper Collection WITH CDs

FABER *ff* MUSIC

To buy Faber Music publications or to find out about the full range of titles available
please contact your local music retailer or Faber Music sales enquiries:

Faber Music Ltd, Burnt Mill, Elizabeth Way, Harlow CM20 2HX
Tel: +44 (0) 1279 82 89 82   Fax: +44 (0) 1279 82 89 83
sales@fabermusic.com   fabermusic.com   expressprintmusic.com

ESSENTIAL AUDITION SONGS

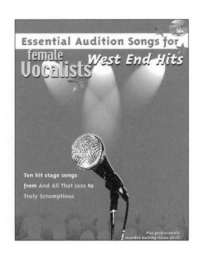

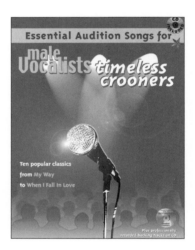

KIDS	**Kids**	MALE	**Broadway**
FEMALE	**Broadway**	MALE	**Pop Ballads**
FEMALE	**Jazz Standards**	MALE	**Timeless Crooners**
FEMALE	**Movie Hits**	MALE & FEMALE	**Comedy Songs**
FEMALE	**Pop Ballads**	MALE & FEMALE	**Duets**
FEMALE	**Pop Divas**	MALE & FEMALE	**Wannabe Pop Stars**
FEMALE	**West End Hits**	MALE & FEMALE	**Love Songs**

FABER ff MUSIC

To buy Faber Music publications or to find out about the full range of titles available
please contact your local music retailer or Faber Music sales enquiries:

Faber Music Ltd, Burnt Mill, Elizabeth Way, Harlow CM20 2HX
Tel: +44 (0) 1279 82 89 82   Fax: +44 (0) 1279 82 89 83
sales@fabermusic.com   fabermusic.com   expressprintmusic.com